Little Jack Horner

The Child's World

Distributed by The Child's World®
1980 Lookout Drive • Mankato, MN 56003-1705
800-599-READ • www.childsworld.com

Acknowledgments
The Child's World®: Mary Berendes, Publishing Director
The Design Lab: Kathleen Petelinsek, Design

Library of Congress Cataloging-in-Publication Data
Petelinsek, Kathleen.
 Little Jack Horner / illustrated by Kathleen Petelinsek.
   p. cm.
 ISBN 978-1-60954-280-1 (library bound: alk. paper)
 1. Nursery rhymes. 2. Children's poetry. [1. Nursery rhymes.] I. Mother
Goose. II. Title.
 PZ8.3.P438Li 2011
 398.8—dc22
 [E]   2010032415

Printed in the United States of America in Mankato, Minnesota.
December 2010
PA02073

ILLUSTRATED BY KATHLEEN PETELINSEK

Little Jack Horner
sat in a corner,

eating his
Christmas pie.

6

He put in
his thumb,

and pulled
out a plum,

and said,
"What a good boy am I!"

ABOUT MOTHER GOOSE

We all remember the Mother Goose nursery rhymes we learned as children. But who was Mother Goose, anyway? Did she even exist? The answer is . . . we don't know! Many different tales surround this famous name.

Some people think she might be based on Goose-footed Bertha, a kindly old woman in French legend who told stories to children. The inspiration for this legend might have been Queen Bertha of France, who died in 783 and whose son Charlemagne ruled much of Europe. Queen Bertha was called Big-footed Bertha or Queen Goosefoot because one foot was larger than the other.

The name "Mother Goose" first appeared in Charles Perrault's *Les Contes de ma Mère l'Oye* ("Tales of My Mother Goose"), published in France in 1697. This was a collection of fairy tales including "Cinderella" and "Sleeping Beauty"—but these were stories, not poems. The first published Mother Goose nursery rhymes appeared in England in 1781, as *Mother Goose's Melody; or Sonnets for the Cradle*. But some of the verses themselves are hundreds of years old, passed along by word of mouth.

Although we don't really know the origins of Mother Goose or her nursery rhymes, we *do* know that these timeless verses are beloved by children everywhere!

ABOUT THE ILLUSTRATOR

Kathleen Petelinsek grew up in Wisconsin where she studied art at the University of Wisconsin. Ever since she was young, she has loved to draw and paint. She has been illustrating and designing children's books for fourteen years. She now lives in Minnesota and Christmas is her favorite time of year. She celebrates the holiday by eating Christmas pie with her husband Dale; her two daughters, Leah and Anna; her two dogs, Gary and Rex; and her kitten, Emma.